T0157828

A TROUBLED MAN
WITH A VIOLENT PAST.

Daniel Buck-Burgoon

AuthorHouse™
1663 Liberty Drive
Bloomington, IN 47403
www.authorhouse.com
Phone: 1-800-839-8640

© 2011 Daniel Buck-Burgoon. All rights reserved.

No part of this book may be reproduced, stored in
a retrieval system, or transmitted by any means
without the written permission of the author.

First published by AuthorHouse 3/25/2011

ISBN: 978-1-4567-5722-9 (e)
ISBN: 978-1-4567-5723-6 (sc)

Library of Congress Control Number: 2011904500

Printed in the United States of America

Any people depicted in stock imagery provided by Thinkstock are models,
and such images are being used for illustrative purposes only.
Certain stock imagery © Thinkstock.

This book is printed on acid-free paper.

Because of the dynamic nature of the Internet, any web addresses or
links contained in this book may have changed since publication and
may no longer be valid. The views expressed in this work are solely those
of the author and do not necessarily reflect the views of the publisher,
and the publisher hereby disclaims any responsibility for them.

I am dedicating this fiction novel to Michael Castro my mate for life. He has helped me so much with this book. I love to write short stories I make up to have fun and not for profit or fame. If that comes down the road so be it. So I hope you enjoy this book. It has a lot of graphic nature so beware.

Sincerely,

Daniel Buck-Burgoon

just an author in 2011 and counting...

THE INCIDENT

I killed a man. His name was Brian Lawrence Smith and he didn't deserve it. The incident was very fast and violent. I swiftly grabbed a ball bat and started swinging viciously and violently with all of my might. Blow after blow I wailed him until he lie still not moving. The police came to arrest me and I told then every detail of how the incident had occurred. We started to tussle then I had got a hold of a baseball bat and did the damage. The incident was ugly and gruesome and I had no place in society with the sin I had committed. I knew I was in hot water and would be for a very long time because of the incident.

1957

I was born on January 7th 1948 in Chicago Illinois to Sherry Anna Jenks. My father was killed in a plane crash transporting supplies to Chili from the U.S. when I was six months old. His name was Joseph Clark Potter. We were a small family being just my mother and I were involved with a small Christian church that helped a lot of war veterans that needed assistance. Anything from food to clothing the church would try and help. We had a lot of cold winters and the months sometimes went by very slowly. The year was now 1957 and I was a young boy in need of a father figure with no guidance. My first taste of trouble came to me at an early age. I was caught for stealing candy form a local market and was let off with a slap on the wrist. The summer came and more trouble would follow me as I should say. I had met a group of boys on the south side of Chicago who said they would take care of me if I did them favors to better them in the long run.

TOPPSIE GREEN

The summer of 1958 I was still running with the same group of boys from the south. Chicago has a lot of different ways it can change a person. The group of boys George, Frankie and Ralph had me dropping off small packages in a neighborhood where I stayed with my mother to older men in fancy automobiles with fancy clothing. The men would pay me money which I gave to Toppsie Green our leader and he took care of us by a cut. I had started to save a bit of money to myself and the other boys knew this. I was a ten year old drug delivery boy. I never knew what was exactly in those packages but I had an idea. One day other boys had seen me coming out of a soda shop and confronted me because they had seen me buy a drink with the money I was making. They had told me to give them my money or be beat up. I refused and they beat the crap out of me. When Toppsie Green found out he assembled his gang and the hunt was on. I never saw what happened but was told that Toppsie and three other boys had found the robbers. Two out of the three boys who beat me had suffered severe head injuries and the third needed eight stitches to his stomach from a knife wound. Toppsie Green assured me I would never be toyed with as long as I was with his gang.

THE PALE FACED MAN

During the summer I ran a lot of drops is what we use to call them and made descent money for my mother and I. I had just had my tenth birthday and felt very important. On a hot muggy summer day in Chicago I met a man named Mr. Grencho. Mr. Grencho was a tall man who was well dressed and had the latest car. He had been asking around for a runner to help him on the other side of town and he had a small proposition for my mother and me. We could live in his apartment building cheap and make good money too. I had told my mother of this and she said she would have to talk to Mr. Grencho about circumstances and what it would cost her. My mother had never found out I was a runner and if she ever did I would be punished hardly.

My mother and I discussed the moving option and came to an agreement we would kindly accept. My mother got a new job at a diner and I was still a runner who was making fast cash. I learned how to survive and get myself out of bad situations. My new home seemed humble but had some things that needed to be worked on but Mr. Grencho had agreed to see that they would be taken care of. There was a tenant who was very quiet and always kept to himself named Mr. Seers. Mr. Seers always sketched pictures around the area and posted them on the walls of apartment building. I think he was a basket case personally but nobody really knew or cared. I had always called him (in my mind the Pale faced man) because he was almost invisible and barely noticed. His art on the other hand was remarkable. He once did a quick sketch of my mother and I called a gesture drawing and it was wonderful for a glimpse.

1959 AND 1960

I was growing older and running small amounts of drugs was all I knew. I never had a real job yet but was getting close to the age where I could work in a corner market as a grocery bag boy. I have dealt with thugs and semi important men in the game of the early drug trade. I never had personally touched the stuff and hoped I never would. My mother was doing well and still single. Mr. Grencho had me on his private payroll and I was saving some amount of cash slowly but surely. My schooling was simple to me because I applied my brain to the fullest extent. I was achieving exemplary marks that suited my mother who was proud of me. My mother hardly talked about my father who had died when I was an infant. I guess the pain was hard for her because I never had the pleasure of knowing him. I was a twelve year old bastard who had wished my father was around for me. I thought of him occasionally but you can't be in pain to much if you never knew the person who you were told did so much good in life for others. The fall of 1960 I ran for Mr. Grencho and became somewhat friends with the man. In a way a dope dealer is really never your friend just a source of income and an acquaintance. The end of 1960 was a bad year for me I had an accident that had broke my ankle. I was climbing a ladder to help the maintenance man of our apartment building to fix a broken window that Mr. Seers had broken throwing a canned food item through. I caught my footing the wrong way and slipped falling three stories cleanly snapping my left ankle. I spent a month and a half in a cast and on crutches hobbling around. It was very difficult but I managed to get through it.

MR. GRENCHO'S DEATH

A year in to 1961 was evolutional and extreme to me because everything was growing and people were changing. Mr. Grencho had been in the business of drugs and it was catching up with him. People started to talk more and were greedier and it was showing fast. One night in 1961 I had heard arguing coming from Mr. Grencho's apartment. I got dressed against my mothers will to see what was the matter. As I approached his apartment the door sprang open and I jumped in to a hall corner as I pier my head around the corner to see the commotion. Mr. Grencho was fist fighting with two other men who were starting to get the best of him. One shaggy man pulled out a knife and stabbed him several times in the chest and stomach. The two men ran my way and right past me as I balled up in the hall way corner scared to death. When they were finally gone I ran to Mr. Grencho's aid as he lie there bleeding and in agony moaning.

I remember right before he died him mustering to me 24 36 19. I had no idea what it meant and would never find out either. I told the officers what I saw and my mother and I with most of the tenants were questioned for several hours. As the flurry of a crowd was broken I felt like crap now I had lost my running gig and Mr. Grencho was gone forever. My mother had never found that I ran for Mr. Grencho and I guess that was positive. I always suspected she had a hunch. Mr. Grencho had a lot of people show for his funeral. People I had never see before.

One man at the funeral had asked me if Mr. Grencho had ever given me a set of numbers and I said yes. I told the man the numbers and he said he would reward me at a later time. He gave me a phone number to reach him if there was anything I ever needed. He had also told me Mr. Grencho's death would be avenged and he had an idea who had done it. I asked the man why are you telling this information to me. He said one day when the time was right I would know. I thought a lot about the horrible things I saw that night and they bothered me but I tried not to show my heartache too badly.

A REAL JOB

1963 was finally here and I was young, healthy, alive and drug running free. I had got a part time job after school an a nearby grocery store as a bagging boy. My job was easy to me and I felt responsible. My life was coming together but there were a lot of year ahead of my life to show all the mistakes I would make that would haunt me. I worked after school went home and tried to stay away from the bad crowds of south Chicago. On an occasion I would here shooting and see some fist fights but stayed away as far as I could. My job my mom and my schooling was most important to me in my current life. I really didn't have many friends just other people I knew from work and school. My boss was kind of a jerk but I dealt with it the best way I knew how and kept my mouth shut. I was making an honest way of life and staying away from trouble. When I got up in the morning I had a routine of school, work, home and did it all over again like clockwork. The summer was coming and my mother and I had planned a trip to Florida to sight see on a bus for two weeks then we would come back home for the remainder of the summer. The time was growing close to our trip and I grew anxious. I worked to have plenty of clean money I earned for the trip to buy souvenirs.

FLORIDA

The bus ride to Florida was the longest trip ever for me as far as traveling goes. This was the first time I had ever traveled out of the state of Illinois. I saw very interesting sights and smelled a lot of bad feet on that bus and I assure you I would never do it ever again. We got to Miami in a few days and had a blast. I had bought a small camera at a pawn shop and a roll of film too. My mother and I did a lot of fun things like go to a small traveling carnival and ate gator jerky. I really didn't care for the gator jerky but did it to say I did it. A week had passed and we were staying at a raggedy motel on the outskirts of Miami. Our money was growing short because of the cab rides so we had to savor as much as we could. I saw a man one day on a corner in downtown Miami. He was begging for change so I threw him a few coins. It isn't any different than home in Chicago where you see it on a daily basis. I had thought he was hungry and if I could help some body I would because it's in my nature. After the two weeks of screwing around on summer vacation we got back on the bus and started our journey home to Illinois. Chicago was home and I was on my way.

1964

1964 and I just had my sweet sixteenth. My job was long over from the market and I was now getting in to women in high school. My grades were great and I had friends. One day a friend of mine asked me if I wanted to come to a night party at his home. I accepted his invitation and prepared to go with my friend in his automobile on a Saturday night.

At the party there was smoking, drinking, and no adult supervision. A group of older boys had been drinking heavily and were starting to bully freshmen around and I didn't like it. I asked them to knock off their carp and leave. I was kind of small but not afraid of them. One of the boys grabbed me from the behind by the neck and started to try and chock me out. I got my head free for a split second and through a backwards head butt hitting him right smack in the nose. He immediately let go and dropped to the floor.

His friends in shock looked at me not knowing what to do. I struck another bully in the face with a closed fist knocking one of his teeth clean out of his mouth. People scattered every way they could. Some one hit me in the head with a blunt object knocking me to the floor. I don't remember much after that as I went unconscious.

When I woke I was lying in the hospital on a bed with a bandage wrapped around my head in throbbing pain. After a few days in the hospital I was released. I was taken to juvenile hall for assault and battery. I would spend a week in juvenile hall then was released to my mother who would ground me for a month. When I went back to school I was given a bad reputation with a number of other kids who you didn't screw with but I deep down just was trying to do good that turned bad because of alcohol and negligence.

MR. SEERS

I did odd jobs to help my mother while she worked at the diner and it made a difference when the bills came due. My school work was slipping a bit and I worried a lot about the future. What was in store for my mother and me and was she ever going to re-marry. Mr. Grencho had once told me a set of numbers and a man said he had a reward for me so I grew curious. I still had the worn paper with the phone number on it and I was ready to collect. It was now 1966 and I was eighteen. Graduation day was coming in June and I was bugged out over this numbers deal but didn't know what to think of it all. I mustered up the courage one day to call the number and was in total surprise to find out who was on the other end of the phone line.

Mr. Seers is who I was speaking to a couple of apartments down from mine. We talked for a very short while of nothing that made and relevant sense then he asked me for the numbers that were given to me the night Mr. Grencho was killed. I gave him. 24 36 19 and he told me to meet him at ten o'clock in the front of the building. I agreed to be there. He added don't be a second late. I arrived at ten sharp to the front of the building where I was told to be. Mr. Seers was there and handed me a small envelope and said nothing at all to me, then he walked away back in to the building. When I got back to my apartment I opened the envelope to find a key in it. There was a note that said U.S. First Bank of Chicago.

REWARD

I rode my bicycle down to the bank the following morning and spoke with a teller to see what I was supposed to do with the mystery key I had. The lady teller took me to a safety deposit box in a room and I was alone when I opened the box. I found one thousand dollars in cash and a key to a car. There was another note that said " If you got this note something happened to me so what is mine is now yours". I had my confusion over the ordeal but was satisfied. I had wondered where the car was and how I was going to find it.

When I got home Mr. Seers was standing in front of the building once again. He said to me come with me out back and I shall show you what Mr. Grencho is giving you kid. I went out back and to my surprise there was a 1957 thunderbird car hardly driven with no body damage. I stood in shock with my jaw almost dropping to the cement. Mr. Seers walked away and said nothing. Mr. Seers was a very mysterious and quiet man who never said much but I deep down had a feeling he knew a lot of secrets about Mr. Grencho. The thunderbird was a great car and I had just got my license just last week. My mother was stoked over the car and asked a lot of questions so I made a story up to cover myself. I felt on the top of the world. Mr. Grencho's death had it's bad and good moments but I came out on top over the whole deal. I saw a man killed in cold blood and sometimes had nightmares. My mother would have to hold me for comfort for a long while before my nightmares would calm down.

As for Mr. Seers he would remain a very quiet mysterious man who always kept to himself and did not ever cause any trouble. I never attempted to try and bond with Mr. Seers because he seemed a bit awkward and weird to me.

VIETNAM DRAFT

I was drafted to boot camp in 1971 and I would have to leave Chicago to try and help my country fight. I arrived in Saigon with a platoon of troops and was trained well before I left the States. I was trained to defend myself against the enemy and I would do just that. It all was well for a couple of weeks until my first incident of real war. I was on a mission to another camp when the platoon I was in was attacked by heavy gun fire. I hit the ground behind a small bed of rocks and kept my head down trying to make a path so I could fire my weapon. I saw one of the enemy's trying to run to another location for cover when I took aim and fired several rounds from my M-16. I struck him several times and watched him drop to the ground.

Two of the twelve platoon members I was with that day died and I saw the first real carnage of war in my life. I spent several years killing the enemy with no remorse because it's all I knew and what I was trained for. I saw a lot of my brothers fall right in front of my face and it was devastating. I ate, slept, and killed the enemy for a grueling four years because it was all I knew at the time. I saw people blown to pieces by land mines, brothers shot in the face and their brains fall (literally in my lap) and air raids that wiped out brothers to nothing. I was stricken with fear a lot at first but it became a way of life for me to get use to. I only wrote my mother every month but never told her any details of what had gone on in Vietnam.

HONORABLE DISCHARGE

I was going to go home after four years of war and I was glad. The city of Chicago seemed so simple to me (I hoped) when I returned. I would be home to see my mother and hopefully some people I knew like good old Mr. Seers. The year was 1975 and things had changed so much since I left Chicago. My thunderbird was still there and my mom was waiting for me. I had several medals from Vietnam for bravery and some common medals just for being there. I was home and still had a little room which I grew up in so I pinned the medals on my curtains so I could see them. Mr. Seers was still there and alive but the same old person. Quiet and lonely keeping his business to himself. I was now home and I was so glad. I had thought a lot on my flight home if I was ever going to be a normal every day (Joe) because I did so much killing over seas. I would find out down the road if that was going to be true or not.

A BAR BRAWL

I was setteling in with my mother and had got a part time job with a local construction company doing rivets. The work was shakey and a lot of the noise reminded me of gunfire in the was. I knew this was a emotional thing I was going to have to deal with. One night after a days work a couple of us guys went to a local bar for drinks. I was talking to a young lady named Suzanne and hitting it off well. We had a few drinks then we danced to a couple of tunes. Most of my buddies were almost done for the night but I stayed. It was almost twelve pm and I was drunk and horney. Another man approached me from behind and told me that Suzanne was his girl and to get lost. I said screw you she is with me now. The situation escalated so fast it could of made your head spin. The man hit me in the jaw knocking me backwards. I picked myself up and bullrushed him getting him on the ground. We tussled and I finally got on top of him.

I pummled his face over and over. Some body broke a bottle over my head cutting me open. People were in a frenzy screaming and egging the fight on. Chairs were thrown and punches were too.

The cops showed up to break the brawl up and people were detained and given citations. I got stitches and the man left under his own will all bruised up with small cuts to his face. I would be banned from the bar and would never return.

CONSTRUCTION FALLOUT

In 1978 I was a full time construction worker with a new girlfriend named "Cathy". When I was finally able to save enough money I got my own apartment across town from my mom and was now independent. I made time for Cathy who had just got out of a bad relationship and was now with me. My job was tough and the war still bothered me so I took my aggressions out on my hard work. All the body's I had stacked up is what I make believed I was doing when I was hitting steel and riveting. On a cold winter day my boss was directing a piece of large steel when the cable snapped. The steel fell nine stories and hit him dead smack on top of his head smashing him like a plump grape DEAD. There was not a thing in the world that could bring him back or save him. The construction fall out was the worst accident I had witnessed in the states since Mr. Grencho's death. I would say I had seen a lot of death and in general it was to much for a person to endure in ten lifetimes.

CATHY SMITS

Cathy was a thirty year old women with no children and a great personality. She had great cooking skills and made a mean lasagna that was spicy. We spent a lot of time at my place hanging out and having sex. We loved each other and I had hoped we were going places. I barely knew much about her family but that didn't really bother me. The year was 1979 I was happy and my mom was doing well. I was with Cathy and we were now a couple who were needing to succeed in the future by making enough money for the future if we were going to raise a family. We started to supplement our income by selling marijuana. We never touched the stuff. Cathy had connections I didn't know about from her past and I was willing to go for the deal to sell the stuff. I never had the slightest suspicion that my girl could have such a connection but life throws a twist at you anyway it can if you don't expect it. Cathy and I started to deal and made good money. All sorts of different people were showing up at all hours of the night and it was getting annoying. We were starting to become very well paid for dealing drugs and I started to get paranoid.

1980 AND 1981

Cathy and I had finally moved to a small house on the south side of Chicago close to where I grew up as a small child. I one day after being in our house for a short period of time ran in to a fellow I vaguely remembered by the last name of Green. Mr. Green was dressed in a three piece suit and had a lot of flashy jewelry. His shoes must of cost a fortune and he was quite a large man. He must of stood six foot five inches tall and had dark black skin. His hair was fancy and he smelled of expensive cologne. Mr Green was coming out of a small pharmacy with a little girl and his wife I assumed. I gathered the courage to ask him if he ever knew a Ms Potter and he said vaguely. He told me he was a very busy man and had to be on his way. He hopped in to a newer Cadillac and sped away. Cathy was at home and I needed to be on my way also.

I knew deep down that man was Toppsie Green from the neighborhood I grew up with him as a kid. I continued to stay away from trouble for many years for the sake of Cathy and me. 1981 was a good year for me Cathy and I now owned our house but the neighborhood was getting worse by the day. One day I hoped to get the hell out of Illinois and away from Chicago. It would never work out that way in the future. I would get in to more trouble over a silly thing that would cost me my freedom.

THE BAD DREAMS FOR ME

As my days went on the war slowly got to me in the form of dreams. I dreamed of gut ripping slaughtering deaths that involved a variety of forms. One dream was a buddy of mine was standing beside me and I looked at him then turned away for a split second. I turned back and his flesh was melting off his head on fire with maggots crawling all over his skin. Another was I hit a land mine with a stick from a distance. The shrapnel came towards me. I saw it in slow motion as it came at my face. I was frozen in place as the shrapnel tore my head to pieces and I actually felt the pain. The dreams were amazingly so real to me and I needed help to try and slow them down. Cathy did what my mother did when Mr. Grencho died and that was hold me but it didn't matter much. I had seen so much pain in life I wish I was dead or I could kill somebody myself to get all the anger of life in my head and aggression out of me. I don't know if that makes much sense to you but it makes perfect sense to me.

THE COPS

The Chicago police were a big factor where I once lived. One night I was in down town Chicago I was pulled over for a lane violation. I had not switched my blinker on to turn a corner. The cops were questioning me over a liquor store robbery and I told them I knew nothing about it. They insisted they run me in for more serious questions and fingerprints. I said what the fuck man I already told you I don't know shit! They insisted on grabbing me and throwing me in the back of the car and beat me up a little. They never took me down to the police station they just beat me up and dropped me off in an alley six blocks away. I went to a corner phone and called 911 for help.

I was once again in the emergency room receiving treatment for abrasions to my face and arms. My car was towed and I had to pay to get it out of impound a few days later. The Chicago cops let me have a good dose of crookedness that night and there was not a thing that I could do about it. I would of killed them if I had my pistol with me that night and made sure I put an extra bullet in each of there damn heads!

THE MID 80'S

The mid 80's were very wild and extreme. The clothing was wild and fads were just coming out. I felt out of place so I stuck to the 70's style clothing. Cathy and I were still together and were getting older but still loved each other. Cathy took to the 80's like wildfire and started doing drugs. I really didn't approve of this but she was her own person. I was always on the edge and I needed to take something to stay off the edge so I started taking pills that were addictive. I took vicodin and soma to calm my nerves. I was addicted to pain killers and Cathy was addicted to methadone pills. Drugs were an everyday thing for a long while and a part of life. The mid 80's were a spoof of a fad because things faded very quickly but the drugs stayed with us for a long while.

1987

The year was now 1987 and I was now the age of 39. My mother was ill from the cancer and I had to take care of her. I was still living on the edge from pills I was addicted to and feeling very paranoid from my post dramatic syndrome I was diagnosed with from the war. I had to get my shit together so my mom could feel better since her cancer was a for certain death. The cancer was in her blood and was spreading fast so I had to be there for her. Cathy had been hooked for some time to methadone pills and she looked like crap. The pain of life was getting worse day to day and I needed a solution to make quick money for my mother's medical bills and two drug habits. I never picked any drug habits up from the war so I guess that was a plus. My mother was sick almost every day with vomiting and nausea and had an occasional fever spell from her sickness. I was there for her every moment to try and comfort her when she needed me and it lasted over four and a half months until she passed away on July 5th 1987.

THE FUNERAL

My mother didn't really have many friends, mostly people who knew her from her old job and very few family members. Mr. Seers showed at the funeral but said nothing to me the whole time nor even wept. The ceremony was fairly short but had a small twist. At the end of the ceremony Mr. Seers went to the open casket and left a ruby red rose in the casket with something that looked like an envelope. It's funny how Mr. Seers never said anything and but always did very mysterious things without a peep. I swear he was a silent angel because when I took the envelope with my name on it the envelope contained a check made out to me for thirty grand. I literally shit myself on the spot. When I turned to see if Mr. Seers was anywhere he had vanished in to thin air. I felt bad for a long time over my mothers death and really would never get over it.

A DEAD MAN

When I was going through my mother's things I had to thank Mr. Seers for helping me so much. I walked down the hall to his apartment to see if he would talk to me. I knocked on the door which was ajar and slowly pushed it open. To my surprise nobody or nothing was there. I walked down to the managers office to ask where Mr. Seers was. I got very chilling news that would stun me and I would never forget it in my lifetime. The manager had told me that there has never been a Mr. Seers living there ever in there records. I questioned more about the apartments records and had found out that apartment has been empty for the last eleven years. I argued the case and was told the same thing over and over. I couldn't believe it, I had been talking to a ghost. I did research on Mr. Seers and found that he had been deceased for thirty seven years and was never living at that specific apartment building. He lived across the street where a house once stood that had burned to the ground thirty seven years ago. I was very confused and had mixed feelings about the situation. Who the hell was I talking with and who did I see. I never made physical contact with Mr. Seers so I guess he really wasn't there, but again he really was.

MR. GRENCHO'S AVENGERS

I was told at Mr. Grencho's funeral many years ago that his death would be avenged. A man had asked me for a set of numbers that I gave to him. The man got in contact with me through a source which I had no idea of where. The man told me he was Mr. Grencho's older brother and he had finally tracked the two me who had killed his brother years ago. He also had told me he knew I was a veteran who could kill and offered me a chance to make big dollars and get away clean. Mr. Grencho's brother said he would make sure he could cover up the hit he offered to me and would pay me big. I said I would take a week to consider his offer. After a weeks worth of hard thinking I accepted. The plot was to whack them in separate places where they lived and he would make the arrangements. He would supply throw away murder weapons for the two hits and dispose of them too.

THE HITS

I was driven to a place in Chicago where the first man lived. He lived in an upscale neighborhood but his house was isolated from the others. I crept up through the side of his house and saw the man watching television sitting on a leather sofa. I pier through a small window in the kitchen then went on the ground creeping up to the sliding glass door. I used a small pocket mirror so it would be hard for him to see me. He got up to go to the kitchen for something during a commercial. I slipped through the glass door and hid behind the sofa staying still. The man returned and started to eat something. I had a thirty eight caliber pistol and a piano cord with two pieces of wood attached to it. I had a choice. Blow his brains out or strangle him to death. I slowly rose from behind the couch and with a quick motion I put the piano cord around his neck chocking him hard and violently with everything I had. The man gasped for air but got nothing but more vice. The more and more I pulled he slipped in to darkness until he stopped moving. I chocked him for two minutes more after he stopped moving to make sure he was gone. After he was dead I wanted to make sure so I shot him in the back of his head six times until I emptied the revolver. It was messy but my first task was complete.

HIT #2

The second hit was even messier. I was driven to a run down motel in town and was told where the second man stayed. I knocked on the door and said it was the manager and he had a message. I bull rushed my way in when the door was open and quickly subdued the man with zip ties. I used the same pistol from the first hit to bully him and make him do what I wanted. After he was immobile and tied up I tortured the man by cutting his limbs and rubbing salt deep in to them. Nobody could here his screams because I had gagged him with a rag and duct tape. I was growing board with the torture so I cut his throat slowly and rubbed salt in it. I pulled out his toe nails slowly then shot him under the chin twice, twice in the chest, and twice in his balls and dick. I walked out of the motel like nothing ever happened and really didn't think much of it. I had done my job and now was ready to collect what was owed to me. I was the avenger of the two men who had brutally killed a man who was doing me good many years ago and I felt one day I might catch the two men who had done it and I did.

THE PAYOFF

For the two jobs I pulled I took in over two hundred and fifty thousand dollars and was living it up. I checked Cathy and myself in to rehab to rid ourselves of our drug addictions. The rehab ate up a lot of my money for the hits but no one ever knew of this, not even Cathy. Cathy never questioned how I made my money she just kept her mouth closed. After three long weeks of rehab we were pill free and feeling great. I still had plenty of cash so I bought a sport car and bought Cathy a diamond tennis bracelet that she always wanted. I put food on the table every day with the money I had and showed off my new Porsche sports car. The years were coming fast and time seemed to fly by. I met a man at a high class hotel I had stayed at with Cathy one night who said he knew me and he seemed very familiar. The man was very tall but thin as a rail and dressed very well. He was sipping on a margarita and we talked for a short while. The man identified himself as Maurice Green aka Toppsie Green. I couldn't believe who I was speaking with. I fired question after question and was overwhelmed by my happiness. Maurice Green was a wealthy business man who had lost a lot of weight since I had seen him at the drug store many years ago. I told him I got lucky on the lottery and that's how I had money. I knew I was lying my ass off but didn't want to come off as a pushover.

A NEW CAREER

I had the opportunity to do something with my life for once that mattered. Maurice had offered me a small position with him at his bank in Chicago. I had to be on my best behavior and get my mind away from criminal acts and not try and steal but make an honest living. He offered Cathy a secretary position effective immediately. When Monday was here we both got ready and headed for the bank to start work. I was a bank teller and Cathy helped people with loans and credit. We were trained for a week and Maurice made sure we were trained properly. I was happy and Cathy was too. The year was 1993 and business was booming for the bank. We worked ten hour days then went home to rest then did the same routine all over again. I was a hard worker and Cathy was a hard worked too. We together pulled in ninety thousand dollars a year between the two of us. Maurice spent a lot of time away from the bank since he owned it. He traveled a lot and had did a one eighty from a street thug to the owner of a small bank. Maurice is a story to be told that would never to be forgotten because it's remarkable. I spent a lot of time at the bank passing out all that cash from hand to hand. I got less temptation to steal so I remained honest. I was living well and I knew it. Cathy was living well too.

NEW HOUSE

Cathy and I were ready to move on from our old smaller house to a bigger one in a nicer part of town. We put the small house on the market and it sold in a month. The family who bought it was happy and we were glad. Cathy and I moved to a bigger upper scale place in Chicago where there was less commotion with crime. The shopping centers were better and had more quality products to buy. We had a lot of the time buy generic items to save money and there was nothing wrong with that. Our new place smelled better and had nicer scenery. The people seemed more stuck-up but I dealt with it. It took us three weeks to settle since we really didn't have much but that would change in time. Cathy was allergic to some of the flowers around the new place so I had to remove them.

I really enjoy living the way I did and I enjoyed not hearing gunshots and police cars also. The war was still in my subconscious but not enough to bother me. The house was too quiet to me sometimes so I watched old war movies on cable television to pass time. I really don't know if that was to wise because it sometimes brought back memories of the war and my buddies that died by my side.

CONFUSION'S

I started having weird feelings with the stress's of life in general. Cathy's drug habit was getting more expensive by the day and slowly draining the money I had in the bank. My personal habit was becoming very abusing towards my health too. I was starting to hate life! I was tired of Cathy and I had a suspicion she was having an affair but couldn't prove a thing. I had questioned her several times but she denied it. She had claimed that she was innocent. One day I ran around town to pay some general bills for the house I came back to my house and found a very interesting item while taking a shower. I found another males pair of under were on the top of the hamper pile that weren't mine. That seriously pissed me off but I kept my feelings inside of me. I was going to wait for the right time and place to deal with the issue. I never had thought I was going to be played a fool of by the women I had loved and it hurt. I one day would find out the truth and hopefully why?

DINNER AT MEL'S

One night Cathy and I were at a little eatery named Mel's near the house. Mel's had the best Italian food in town in my opinion. We ate and laughed for hours and hours. I had started asking all sorts of questions (while she was drunk) about her ex-boyfriends and lovers. She sure could hole her liquor because I couldn't get the little bitch to crack. My plan had been to get her drunk then see if I could get her to give up the mystery man who I knew was in our house because of the under ware that weren't mine. The night came to an end and I never got anything from her worth using for my case against her. I would find out slowly but surely who this man was and beat the shit out of him one day I hoped. I drove us home and our magical night was over. Before I fell asleep a lot of negative shit had passed through my mind and I went to sleep pissed but kept it to myself.

BANK ROBBERY

I went to work on April 19th 1994 and that day would
be a nightmare. That morning at work everything
was smooth until ten thirty am. Three men in ski
mask stormed in the bank waving hand guns around
ordering everybody to the floor. The guard on duty
"Charles" was quickly overpowered and disarmed.
I hit the floor and covered my head thinking what
to do. The robbers never saw me hide because I saw
them right before they stormed in the bank. The panic
button was out of my reach and I was curled against
the back of the teller desk. I heard one of the men climb
over the counter and go towards the teller drawers
grabbing cash from them at random. He must of not
have seen me balled up under the counter so when
he came my way I stuck my foot out and tripped him
knocking him in to a women teller named "Carol" and
he fell over her. I had to think fast so I sprang out of
my curled up ball and wrestled him until I got his gun

away from him. I didn't see but one of the robbers shot at me striking me in the shoulder. I stumbled back and returned fire hitting the robber in his chest. The third robber opened fire at me wildly missing three times as I hit the floor and pushing the panic button which alarmed the police that there was a robbery in progress.

The robber I tripped stayed still as I lie on the floor holding the pistol at him. I told him if he moved I would kill him. He froze and did not move a muscle. The only robber standing fled empty handed. The whole robbery only lasted fifty five seconds or so before it was over. I received treatment for a bullet wound to my shoulder but was going to be ok. When Mr. Green had found out what I had done he was pleased to here I foiled the robbery. As for the robber I shot in the exchange of gunfire, he later died at the hospital and I had got away with a clean slate because I was a small time hero. My story was in the news and I felt very happy for what I did for those people that day in the bank and saved a lot of lives too.

RELATIONSHIP TROUBLES

Cathy and I had been together a long time but were never married. We had friction from time to time like a relationship has but no blow-ups. I had found out through a source of mine she was secretly having an affair and lying to me. So I confronted her about it. She did not deny that she was having an affair and I wanted to break things off. I would have no part with a cheating lying bitch who didn't love me. I was pissed but was mature about the circumstances of the break up and was willing to split everything we owned down the middle. I was heart broken but managed to get through a lot worse things in my forty years plus in life because she really didn't know shit when it came to pain and suffering. I have had buddies faces explode right next to me and their brain matter end up all over my vest and pants in Nam. It was over I would give her the house and I would end up back in south Chicago. I had quit my job because she still worked at the bank and I had hundreds of thousands of dollars saved in the bank. We were through I was done and I just didn't care about anything anymore. I got very lonely fast and I was starting to talk to myself when nobody was there. Was I going Crazy?

VOICES

I was living alone and slowly going insane. I worked out
a lot with sit- ups and push-ups and slept weird hours. I
took long jogs at three in the morning and broke in cold
sweats from war dreams. I stared at the walls for hours
and saw shapes that weren't really there. And I heard
voices. I lived in a run down place with cockroaches
and it smelled bad from the garbage I never cleaned up.
The voices grew worse day by day and I felt depressed
and useless in this cold world. The voices is who I talked
to and they had demon written all over them. I believed
in God but he wasn't helping me. I gave up on praying
to him because he didn't answer my prayers. I stayed
isolated for months at a time and associated with no
one. I hated everybody and everybody hated me I
believed. The demons were the answer to my problems.
I had lots of fits of angry rages and destroyed my stuff
then bought new. I could never have thought I could
ever sink this low in life but it was now reality.

A SHRINK FOR ME

I went to a head doctor to try and better myself. We had deep sessions about everything I could possibly think of and was totally honest. I spent five days a week for an hour a day in therapy trying to get help. I was in therapy for three months before I snapped on my therapist. He set me off digging on a touchy subject and I went off on him. I warned him to back off but he ran his mouth so I got angry and attacked him. I punched him in the face several times breaking his nose and jaw. I also broke his wrist when he tried to defend himself against one of my blows. I was arrested and put in jail immediately.

JAIL

I was sentenced to six weeks in the Chicago county jail for assault and battery. I spent a lot of time exercising and watching television with the other inmates. I didn't get in to any fist fights there just a couple of minor arguments from people begging for my commissary stash. I shared with those who weren't assholes to me and stayed away from trouble due to the fact of getting in trouble would stack up more time. I wasn't afraid of jail nor anybody in it. I did my six weeks of jail time and paid restitution to my shrink for his medical bills and it was over. I now had a felony on my record and a bad past that would continue to haunt me for the rest of my life.

A RUN IN

A few weeks out of jail I stopped in a corner bar close to the motel I was staying at. I had a run in with Maurice Green the banker. I asked him what he was doing in this part of town? He answered I grew up here with my old gang don't you remember. I saw that he had a few drinks and was rambling on about how Cathy was stealing money and had been fired by him personally. I got a grin from ear to ear. I said "That bitch got what she deserves". I walked away from Maurice and left the bar to go home for the night happy as hell. I knew one day Cathy would dig her own grave and have to bury herself. After that run, in I never saw Maurice "Toppsie" Green ever again.

THE CITY PARK

I usually did some jogging in a near by city park. I also did some fishing too. I had quite a bit of money still saved from my earlier days and bought only what I needed for myself. I tried therapy and that was a waste. The year was 1998 and I was fifty years old but in great shape. The park was peaceful to me so I spent a lot of time there alone. I fished tried to play ball and drove golf balls for distance. I was horrible at basketball but could move quicker than most of the younger generation. I was in shape with my exercising and started to interact with people out doors more often. I didn't care what there names were I just wanted to be physical and stay out of trouble.

The park was an outlet I had managed to use to get out my frustrations and anger. I like to blow off steam and sweat so I went to the park to do just that. I also enjoyed the scenery of the park. It was an open public place that was free for anybody to use. Sometimes I would take napes during the day then go home to eat my supper. My hours of sleep improved and the weird hours turned to more normal times.

OLD AGE

I felt a lot of aches and pains all over my body. I was getting old but still had my mind. My IQ was above one thirty and it showed in school and on the streets growing up. I was never really afraid of anything after the war because I believed everybody will die one day and it didn't scare either. I felt in shape but my knees popped when I bent them and my elbows popped too. I was an older man with no children and had never been married. Cathy was once the love of my life but she decided to cheat on me so we broke it off several years ago. I knew I was never going to have children and did not care. Kids are needy is what I always said. I was a bitter man with a fucked up background so I had to live with me. I was hard on myself a lot when I use to make a mistake but that feeling was gone a long time ago. Old age is a thing everyone will go through if you live long enough to get there. Believe it!

HOSPITAL STAY

I was tired of life and my doctor suggested that I check in to a mental hospital for a few days to see if it could help me and let the doctors observe me. I saw people in the hospital with all sorts of different problems and the ages varied from younger to older. I was one of the older patients there who kept a cool head with my private sessions and did the group sessions like I was suppose to. I started to take a pill called haloperidol for schizophrenia which I was diagnosed with. I understood what the diagnosis was because I had read about it in medical magazines. I liked to read medical magazines for leisure and gathered a lot of information form them. My medicine was taking effect on me very quickly and making me very tired and lethargic. I paid to stay an extra week in the hospital to see if I could better myself. I met people with bi-polar disorders and even people who had tourettes syndrome. The conditions of some of the patients were minor to severe but everybody was similar in some kind of way. Every one there was trying to get themselves better that's why they were there. The hospital was a free come and go ward not a mandatory one. There were other vets there with similar issues to mine.

I stayed a total of ten days at the mental hospital before I checked myself out and was on a drug called Haldol. The drug made me feel a little more sane and alert to reality.

HALDOL EFFECTS

The haldol made me stiff as a rock. I went to a specialist to see if there was something I could do to help the stiffening effects ease up. The doctor put me on a little white pill named cogentin which was a muscle relaxer. The haldol and cogentin combined was doing the right thing for me because I felt like a normal human for once (after the war). My bad dreams slowly went away and I felt very calm and peaceful for once in my life. I did my daily routine of exercises and jogging in the park. I finally picked all the garbage up from my motel room and replaced the things I had broken in my fits of rages and ate wiser food items too. The pills made me have more feelings that showed. I thought of my war buddies that had died and wept about them. I cried over my mothers death sorrowful and regretfully. I really missed my father I never knew and had wished I had knew him. The pills were making me have so much feelings I felt like a pussy but really did not care because I needed to release my deepest feelings of hurtful pain and suffering. Haldol was a good pill to take for me I guess.

I had always wondered how long it would be for me in life to find my enlightened path and I was going to find out in the next few years of my life what that would be. I really never worried about death coming to me because death didn't scare me because it was a natural part of everyday life and everybody would one day meet their maker some way. I just kept on trying to stay in shape and better myself with every passing day until I would die. I had a favorite passage from Church and it was "Man shall not live by bread alone, but by every word that comes from the mouth of God".

WINTER DAYS

During the Chicago winters I stayed in my motel and read a lot about medicine and how it worked. I read as much material as I could get a hold of. I learned a lot about the human body and how it worked. I had always liked to read magazines ranging from a variety of different subjects but loved medical ones. I kept my place spotless and had three meals a day. I had a small refrigerator in my hotel room which I kept soda and beer in for a cold drink in the middle of the night. I rarely drank water. I had a small bathroom with a stand-up shower and no bathtub. The winters were depressing most of the time so I had to keep myself occupied. The cold weather allowed me to do a lot of working out and I stayed in great shape for a min over fifty years old. I noticed in the mirror a lot where I had been shot in my shoulder during the bank robbery years ago and it was ugly. I just did what I could to pass time before the winter was gone and better weather arrived. Over four months of winter than the coldness was starting to go away. I was doing absolutely nothing with my life and my money was depleting. I needed to do something worth my while so I attempted to work again.

NEW JOB

I got a job bagging groceries just like when I was a boy. Bagging groceries was easy to me so my boss moved me to a cash register position quickly. It looked funny for an old man to be bagging groceries. I worked day in and day out at the grocery store checking customers out. I knew a lot of faces from the store and they knew me also. I was taking my medicine the proper way and working. I felt very responsible and my bills were paid on time when they were due. The job was just what I wanted, close to the motel, descent pay, and I was a satisfied man. I liked the new job a lot but every job comes with it's fair share of assholes. You just have to learn how to deal with them in a nice manner because I was told the customer was always right. Deep down I knew that wasn't true because if a customer gave you a ten and back from five dollars and he or she knew they had to much and said nothing your drawer would come up short. The cashier would be penalized.

I did my work and tried to not make any mistakes. My boss was cool and very lenient. I took breaks with other employees to eat and to have conversations about what ever. I had a simple life now that was very pleasing to me. My job was a great chance for me to get my life in order and if I stayed on track I would hopefully stay out of trouble with other people in general.

I had an idea of maybe one day becoming assistant manager at the grocery store and when the time was right I would approach my boss for the position. I knew I would have to work hard and be there a while before the time was right to ask my boss the question.

PIZZA PARLOR

I was eating a small pizza at a round table pizza joint in town when a group of kids came in. I could tell they were teens and were acting very rowdy and obnoxious. One of the teens threw a balled up straw paper at me and I asked him to knock off his shit. He started cussing at me calling me out side to "throw down". There was three teens total and I was getting pissed off at them. I tried to blow them off when one of them grabbed my cap and ran outside. I stood up and stormed out wanting my cap back. One teen punched me in the back of the head jolting me forward in to one of the teens. I immediately grabbed the young boy by his throat and started to choke the life out of him. The other two teens started beating the shit out of me when I fell to the ground on top of their friend still choking him. He had passed out and I tried to get to my feet. I never got the chance to get up before other people broke up the squabble. The boy I choked gained consciousness and was gasping for air. I was sitting on my butt holding my ribs and the boy I had choked got up and ran off with the other two boys.

The cops came and asked questions of how they looked and what went down during the attack. I told them everything I could remember and was released. As I walked to my motel I had realized I was not a bad ass soldier any more and was just an old fart. I got over the attack quickly and was back at work the next day. My ribs hurt so I asked my boss for a sick day and he said take two. He would call somebody to cover my shifts for the next two days.

TWO DAYS AT HOME

My two sick days I caught up on much needed sleep. I stayed away from the pizza parlor because of the teens that had attacked me. I mostly read my magazines and watched my television. I rented a few porno's for my sexual pleasure and took jogs before the sun went down. I was plenty board so I walked to the liquor store to browse the magazine sections looking for reading material. During my time home I met a man who needed to borrow a few bucks for his groceries so I lent him a few dollars probably to never see him again. The two days were almost up and I was to return to work. I thanked my boss for the time off and he told me your welcome.

THE MONEY MAN

The man who I lent money to somehow knew I worked at the local market. I told him I couldn't talk to him at work so I had to send him on his way. After work he was there waiting for me. I cautiously protected my wallet and gave him a few more dollars and he left the place where I worked. I had very little money as it was so I had to stretch what I had. Day in and day out he tried to bum change and dollar bills from me mostly succeeding. It grew very tiring and I started to grow angry. I one day just told him no more money and he got pissy about it. He must of thought since I was an old man he could take advantage of me. I finally put a cease to the borrowing I knew would never be re paid. I watched my back for several days that turned to several weeks and I even saw his peering around corners following me. The man finally found out where I lived had was even knocking on my front door. I was a bit frightened and had to call the cops to get him to leave.

THE END OF FREEDOM

I went to work and come home as quick as I possibly could. I started having nightmares of the money man killing me. I stopped taking my pills because the man was terrorizing me. I grew very paranoid and scared. The man even went to the trouble of looking through my window in the motel I stayed in. I had had enough of his shit. I bought a Louisville Slugger base ball bat and kept it by my bed side.

One night when I came home from work I had noticed the man following me. I picked up my pace and walked faster and faster. When I got to the motel I fidgeted with my key at the door getting it unlocked quickly. I went inside and locked the door behind me. The man started pounding on my door saying let me in you son of a bitch! I was so scared I called the cops and they said to hold on. The man started to kick in the door so I grabbed the base ball bat and was ready to defend myself. The man pushed in the door and came towards me in a fit of rage like I owed him something. I yelled, stay away or I'll kill you! The man came on anyway. When he got in my range I struck him in the head several times with the bat over and over until he hit the floor. I continued to beat him until he was not moving at all. I hit him in the head a few more times with full force and felt his head split open and saw his skull. The man was dead! And I had killed him! His name was Brien Lawrence Smith and he didn't deserve it. My name is Leroy Charles Potter and I killed a man. Now I have to pay for what I have done.

LAST THOUGHTS
FOR THIS BOOK

I write these short stories to exercise my ability to use my mind. They may be short but they will all have the same thing in common and that is people will do anything in life to survive. I just want the people around me to be proud of me and know that I had accomplished something in life. So I will write on…